The Whatamagump

©2018 Whatamagump, LLC. All Rights Reserved. No part of this
publication may be reproduced, stored in a retrieval system or transmitted
in any form by any means electronic, mechanical, or photocopying,
recording or otherwise without the permission of the author.

For more information, visit:
www.thewhatamagump.com

Printing coordinated by:
Mascot Books
620 Herndon Parkway #320
Herndon, VA 20170
info@mascotbooks.com

Library of Congress Control Number: 2017916075

CPSIA Code: PRTWP1117A
ISBN-13: 978-0-692-93987-1

Printed in Malaysia

Written by **Tyrone Wells**
Produced by **Broken Eagle Studio**

The Whatamagump

There's magic in a Whatamagump
When you say "jump" five times,
"jump, jump, jump, jump, JUMP"
They run and then jump, and are gone in a flash
They fly through the air, and they go CRAZY fast!

Original Whatamagump music and read-along
performed by Tyrone Wells
available on iTunes and at
www.thewhatamagump.com

Julie was brave, so she ran to her door
She gathered her courage while she counted to four
She swung the door open, and what did she see?
A Whatamagump that was scared as could be!

His knees were all shaky, he barely could stand
But he stretched out a flower he held in his hand
He wanted a friend, he wanted some fun
And he thought maybe Julie could be just the one

Julie decided that they would be friends
The Whatamagump had the friendliest grin
He wanted to try to learn to be brave
He hoped maybe Julie could teach him the way

Now the Whatamagump had a very loose tooth,
but he was too scared to tug at its root
Julie was kind, she was gentle but firm
She gave a slight tug on the tooth with a turn

The Whatamagump was afraid of a pea
"Afraid of a pea, now how could that be?

The Whatamagump offered Julie a ride
So she climbed right on up and held on to his sides

She said "Jump!" four times
and then one time more
And off they both flew
to be brave and explore

The Whatamagump saw a bug that was crawling
He was shaking and pointing, he was practically bawling

Julie said, "Bugs just crawl or fly by
They won't hurt you a bit, so just wave and say, 'Hi!'"

The Whatamagump saw a Jink and a Whump
And, worried, he ran and hid by a stump
He whispered to Julie, "They don't look like me
They're purple and blue and talk differently!"

Now, Julie knew that we're not all the same
So she said, "We're all different, and that is OK
The colors we are, the things that we wear,
the way that we talk, the style of our hair

We're all very different, but we're also the same
We all have a heart, a smile, and a name"
She said, "Let's be friends!" to the Jink and the Whump
so they played hide and seek with the Whatamagump

The Whatamagump was afraid of the slide
"Afraid of the slide? NO! Come on and let's ride!

Just climb up the stairs, we're right behind you
Now throw up your hands and scream,
'WHOOPTY WHOO!'"

The Whatamagump saw a shadow behind him
He thought it was scary. Was it coming to find him?
He ran, he jumped, he cried, "Get away!"
But the shadow just followed him, every which way

Julie said something she knew to be true,
"That shadow's not spooky, it's coming from you!
So don't be afraid, you're just blocking the light
We all have a shadow, and that is alright"

The Whatamagump said, "It's past time for bed!
You have to get home to lay down your head!"

So Julie jumped on and back home they both flew
And Julie grew quiet as she stared at the moon

Back at her house, Julie said, "I'm afraid!
If I go to sleep, I won't get to play"
"But we all need to sleep," said the Whatamagump
"If we never did sleep, we'd all be such grumps!"

"Sleep is the way that our bodies renew
If you love to play, it's the best thing you can do!
When you wake up, you'll be ready to go,
to run and to jump, to play and to grow"

"I'll lay down right here, and sleep just beside you
No need to be scared, close your eyes just like I do"
Then the Whatamagump did the silliest thing
Closing his eyes, he started to sing

"Bump, thump, the Whatamagump,
bump, thump, the Whatamagump,
bump, thump, the Whatamagump..."

Before they both knew it, they had fallen asleep
and Julie was dreaming a dream that was sweet
She dreamt that she heard some bumps and a thump

And then made a new friend, called *"the Whatamagump"*

Tyrone Wells
Author, Character & Story Development

Broken Eagle LLC

Bryan McIntyre:
Producer, Lead Set & Prop Fabricator, Sculptor,
Set Dressing, Lighting & Photography

Greg Boettcher:
Art Director, Character & Set Design,
Character Painting, Prop Fabricator, Sculptor,
Set Dressing, Lighting & Photography, Photo Editing

Additional Artists:

Character Sculptors
Bruce Bowman and David Downes with
Geahk Burchill, Charles Daniels, Daniel Miller, Josh Pearce, Mattew Pugh

Prop & Set Fabrication
Bruce Bowman, Chris Caniglia, Lalanya Gunn, Daniel Miller

Character Molding & Casting
Geahk Burchill

Prop & Set Painting
Lois Boettcher, Leigh-Alexandra Jacob

Softgoods
Lisa Chung, Brandy Cochrane, Brandi Wiklund

Costume & Wigs
Brandy Cochrane

Text Layout
Marisa Ghiglieri-Linquist

 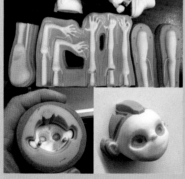 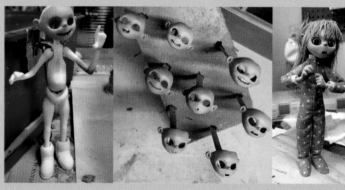 

Many Thanks to our Social Media influencers:
Damien Webb, Maribel Diaz, Jim McKenzie, Steve Ferrera,
Phil Dale, Amber Cunningham, Ryan Thomas Monohan, Ellison Brooks

The Whatamagump began as a brief phone discussion in the summer of 2015 between Tyrone, Bryan and Greg. The idea was simple: Tyrone would write a children's story, and Broken Eagle would handmake all the artwork (instead of drawings, paintings, etc.).

What transpired over the course of the next two years was an incredibly ambitious and exciting journey that included a hugely successful crowdfunding campaign, a musical EP & read-along, and the talents of over a dozen experts in the fields of art and music.

In addition to those who directly helped make the book happen, there are numerous others who contributed in more intangible ways.

Bryan McIntyre would like to thank the following:
Tiffany, Penny & Duncan – you are my whole world. Mom, Dad,
Grandma Jean Duncan, The Newbergs, the Somboonsiris, David & Bethya Becker,
the Laubscher Family, Mark Hartz, Aaron Fountain, Jay Buchanan

Greg Boettcher would like to thank the following:
Lalanya, Mom, Dad, Jeanette, Michael and Sharon, Uncle, The Gunns,
The Other Boettchers, Ian, Matt, Shannon, and all the New Dealers,
the Laika crew, Monty, Jack and Eric

Tyrone would like to thank the following:
Erin, Aria, & Ireland Wells, the Wells Family, the Chang Family

Collectively, Tyrone, Bryan and Greg would like to thank the following:
Mike Barnet, Tyler Bacon, Mark Chipello, Erica Johnson, John Nolan and Chris Ohlgren,
Marisa Ghiglieri-Linquist, Brandon Zedaker, Johnny Jones, Hill family, Amdahl family, Oola,
Yonker family, Maurer family, Naren Aryal & Mascot Books, HouseSpecial, Keith Iluag

KICKSTARTER

a thank you to our backers

Tim Hill
Aaron L. Cohen
HouseSpecial Studio
Abby & Drew Abraham
ad memoriam Melissa Roesch
Addyson Beelman & Papi
AJG & JRP
Alan Crawford
Alana Hollingsworth
Allison Skinner
Alvin & Bonnie Gunn
Amber Cunningham
Amber Ridge & Bill Remling (A+B)
Angela & Scott Newton
Anna Maria Purzynska
Annie Distad
Anonymous
Anthony Licona
April Huang
Arlo Howard Merrick
Ashley Hectus
Ashley Laurén Combs
Ashley Reeves
Avery, Cody, Brooklyn & Presley Murray
Bayne Smart
Bradford Reeves
Brandy M. Hickey
Brenda & Jim Hill
Brent & Heather Stoffer
Brett & Lori Leinard
Brett & Daralynn Wright
Brett Bixby
Carly L. Halm
Caroline V. Allen
Chris & Jessica Patay
Chuck & Jeannie Coder
Cohen Talley + his super cool parents
Colleen Fitzgerald
Crystal M. Borde
Cyndi & Ron Brandt
Dani Weidner
Daniel Liang & Sabrina Chang
Dave Finnell
David & Susan Meyer for Eva Mae
David & Dachene Newman
Debbie Beck-Siddiqui
Debbie Connolly
Debbie Moriarty
Dori Bertino
Ebrahim Al-Bishri
Elaine & Damien
Elaine Jones
Eli S. Morfin
Eliza Chicu
Emme Lovell
Erica Burley
Everly C. Willson

Ezekiel Gunn
Foster & Grace
Gary & Venita Longley
Gary & Chantel Howell
Glenda S Jones
Go Family
Gpa & Roro Noles
Grandma Sexy (aka Tracey Jordan)
Greg & Karla Wanee
Greg Holcombe
Hannah M. Norwood
Henri & Natasha Steenkamp
Hilde Schjerven
Ifly, ML
Jan & Dean Lanouette
JB
Jenn Sruba
Jennifer Powell
Jessica Lee Wisnowski
Jill Openshaw
Jimmie & Amy Bernardi
John Kinsler
Jon & Julie Wright
Jony & Emily Bos
Joshie & Sammie
Justin Owens & family
Katarzyna (Kasia) M. Prouty
Kathie DeLaGarza
Kay & Izzy Garcia
Keith Ilaug
Keith McQueen
Kelly Ostendorf
Ken & Lori Gallagher
Kevin, Leslie & Sfeffany Maxwell
Kimberly Lo
Kirk Kelley
Kristen Llorente - in memory of Steve Pratt
Krystle ("Krystle Dee") Suszter
Laura & Alex Kontoleon
Lauren & Casey Allington
Lexi Danger Farlow
Liliana & Nathaniel Wanee
Lora J. Clements
Makayla & Chloe Davenport
Margalena Lepore
Mariah & Gabriel Bishop
Maribel Diaz
Mark & Heidi Lowe
Mark, Kellen, & Malia Hartz

Mark, Kellen, & Malia Hartz
Michael Behnen
Michael J. Maltese
Michele Newell
Neal & Jenny Gower
Nelson Sung Wo Chang
Nicole Bresnahan
Nolan Smith
Patti Jones
Paula Soulodre (& Tim Shaffer)
Peter Malek
Pine Box Daddy
Reichstein Family
Renee Kingsbury
Robert Melchior
Sarah Barnes
Scotty Tebeau
Scott Schultz
Seth, Mom, Elizabeth, & Gisele Fleischer
Shane O'Neill
Sharon Hylton
Sherri Dawson
Sherwood Choe
Simi
Somboonsiri Family
Stacy J. Lugg
Stella Miellè Lin McGaughy
Stephanie L. Haston
Susanne D. Lubash
Sweet Lil Anna Bee
The Amodio Family
The Boutry's!
The Colby kids
The Colorado Wilsons
The Ellis Family
The LeBleu Family
The Morehead Family
The Schipper Family
The Wilson Family
Tiffany & Tommy Taylor
Tiffany Licona
Tisha & Jason Lehfeldt
Tobi & Joel Nicholson
Tracy Chapman
Vincent & Dana Stegner
Wild Palette Pictures
Wendy Andersen
Margie Murray

Clair Stocks Baca
Alan Sperry
Kimberly Hahn
Michael
Janelle
Ashley Nielsen
jennifer crone
Raegan Cury
Heidi cooper
Christian Falcon
Rebecca Bowen
Barbarita Lopez
Jenn
Scott & Nicole Rainsberr
Katherine Eldean
Rudolph Finamore
Gina Minard-Rivera
Sandra Sefcik
Erin Hetrick
Kim Real O
Katrina Hill
Doug Lada
Mike Gonneville
Julie Cuy
Amy Carmichael
Kevin Zahrndt
Tina Neuwirth
Bailey Hill
Jean Duncan
Mike and Bev McIntyre
Levi Ware
The Fountain Family
Connor Hill
Christina V Boyles
Daniel Liang
Bill Remling
Aaron and Janelle White
Diana Chipello
Jim Palmer
Elaine Nixon
Teryn Smith
Aly Driggers
Lisa Wodtke
Georji Belles Brown
Kristin Schmidt
Jessica Vanderhoff
Tammy Smith
Ashley Sickels
Lori Weech
Dustin Burnett
Cathy Reagan
Adam Alva Lowe
Sarah
Mari Rinta-Piirto
Brandi Laubscher
Danae
Bradley Corrigan

THANK YOU
for making this project possible
we couldnt have done this without you

Tyrone, Bryan , Greg